Loula

is leaving for
Africa

For my sister Martine, who often left for Africa...
and came back five minutes later.

Text and illustrations © 2013 Anne Villeneuve

All rights reserved. No part of this publication may be
reproduced, stored in a retrieval system or transmitted, in any
form or by any means, without the prior written permission
of Kids Can Press Ltd. or, in case of photocopying or
other reprographic copying, a license from The Canadian
Copyright Licensing Agency (Access Copyright). For an
Access Copyright license, visit www.accesscopyright.ca
or call toll free to 1-800-893-5777.

Kids Can Press acknowledges the financial support of
the Government of Ontario, through the Ontario Media
Development Corporation's Ontario Book Initiative; the
Ontario Arts Council; the Canada Council for the Arts;
and the Government of Canada, through the CBF, for
our publishing activity.

Published in Canada by
Kids Can Press Ltd.
25 Dockside Drive
Toronto, ON M5A 0B5

Published in the U.S. by
Kids Can Press Ltd.
2250 Military Road
Tonawanda, NY 14150

www.kidscanpress.com

Kids Can Press is a **C⊙rus**™ Entertainment company

The artwork in this book was rendered in
ink and watercolor.
The text is set in Goldenbook.

Edited by Karen Li and Yasemin Uçar
Designed by Karen Powers

This book is smyth sewn casebound.
Manufactured in Shenzhen, China, in 3/2013
through Asia Pacific Offset

CM 13 0 9 8 7 6 5 4 3 2 1

LIBRARY AND ARCHIVES CANADA CATALOGUING IN PUBLICATION

Villeneuve, Anne

Loula is leaving for Africa / written and illustrated by
Anne Villeneuve.

ISBN 978-1-55453-941-3

I. Title.

PS8593.I3996L68 2013   jC813'.54   C2012-908579-0

Loula
is leaving for
Africa

Written and illustrated by

Anne Villeneuve

KIDS CAN PRESS

Loula is sick and tired of having brothers.

Three MEAN, HORRIBLE, STINKY brothers.

"I've had ENOUGH!" she cries. "I'm leaving."

She takes the essentials ... her cat,
her tea set and her best drawing.

Loula is going far away, very far away, the farthest away she
can get from those TERRIBLE triplets.

"Mama," says Loula, "I'm going to Africa."

"Wonderful," sings her mother while practicing her role for the opera. "Just don't catch a cold."

"Papa," says Loula, "I'm going to Africa."

"Marvelous, my little brussels sprout!" replies her father, busy creating a new mustache. "Just don't come home too late."

"Fine!" Loula exclaims. "Nobody cares about me. I'm never coming back."

"Mademoiselle!" Gilbert exclaims. Gilbert is the family chauffeur. He drives Loula's mother to the opera. "What are you doing up in that tree?"

"This is not a tree," says Loula. "This is AFRICA!"

"Really? I thought Africa was this way."

"Are you sure?" asks Loula.

"Yes. Well, no, we would have to look on a map."

"Do you have one?"

"I think I might," says Gilbert.

"This is an old map, but Africa should be in the same place. You see? Here it is ... AFRICA!"

"Thank you, Gilbert. So long!"

"But Mademoiselle Loula, first you have to
take a ship, or else you will never get to Africa."

"Never?"

"Never."

"Okay then, I'll take a ship," says Loula.

"Good. Do you have your ticket?"

"No ... but I have my best drawing. Will that do?"

"It will do just fine," declares Gilbert.

"Where is the ship?" asks Loula.

"Right here," replies Gilbert. "All aboard!
I hope you don't get seasick."

"Mademoiselle, may I ask, why Africa?"

"Because!" Loula explains. "Africa is far away, very far away, the farthest away I can get from my MEAN, HORRIBLE, STINKY brothers. Plus they are scared of snakes. And if they come, piranhas will eat them."

"Well then," says Gilbert, "I think Africa is the best destination."

"Gilbert, are we there yet?"

"Not yet. Now we have to cross the jungle.
DON'T LOOK UP NOW, Mademoiselle. There is
an enormous snake in that tree. Let's pretend we
don't see him."

"So where is Africa?" asks Loula.

"Maybe it is this way," suggests Gilbert.

"Or maybe that way ..."

"Gilbert, I think we're lost."

"You may be right. What should we do?"

"Look, Gilbert! A giraffe.
Let's ask her the way."

"Good idea, Mademoiselle,
except I don't know how
to speak giraffe."

"Oh, but my cat does!"
exclaims Loula.

"Gilbert! I didn't
know Africa was this far.
I'm hungry."

"Mademoiselle, look! What luck!
Here is a restaurant. Which would you
prefer? Ostrich egg soufflé
or a grasshopper sandwich?"
"Both!" cries Loula.

"Gilbert! We're not so far from Africa now. I see some chimpanzees."

Gilbert nods. "True. We must simply cross this desert."

"Then take a plane ..."

"... and go for a short camel ride."

"Mademoiselle Loula! Look! AFRICA!
It's just a boat ride away."

"Another boat?" asks Loula.

"Yes, but a very comfortable one.
The *Queen Elizabeth 2*."

"Mademoiselle, please! Don't put your hand in the water! Piranhas!"

"Here we are, Mademoiselle, in AFRICA!"

"Now I feel free!" says Loula.

"The long trip has made me thirsty, Mademoiselle.
Would you happen to have some tea?"

"Yes! I do, I do!"

"They say that the nicest sunsets are in Africa," says Gilbert.

"It is so quiet," murmurs Loula.

"Gilbert?"

"Yes, Mademoiselle?"

"Do you think piranhas like to eat mean,
horrible, stinky brothers?"

"I don't know, Mademoiselle Loula.
Wouldn't they be a little hard to digest?"

"I suppose."

"Gilbert?"

"Yes, Mademoiselle?"

"I'm tired," Loula sighs.

"Yes, of course, Mademoiselle.
I will take you home."

"It is not so far away," whispers Gilbert.